Insane Ideas Decaying in a Distasteful Pit:

An Exhumation of Eight Short Stories and Vignettes

Sean Hawker

Copyright © 2021 Sean Hawker

Cover and Book Design by Sean Hawker

Proofread and Edited by Estelle @ PaperTrue

All rights reserved. No part of this publication may be reproduced, distributed, or transmitted in any form or by any means, including photocopying, recording, or other electronic or mechanical methods, without the prior written permission of the author. For permission requests, write to the author at: sean_hawker@hotmail.com.

Paperback Edition

Printed in Great Britain by Amazon

Although every precaution has been taken in the preparation of this book, the publisher and author assume no responsibility for errors or omissions. Neither is any liability assumed for damages resulting from the use of information contained herein.

FOR ELLA

LET YOUR IMAGINATION RUN WILD.

(BY THE WAY, YOUR DADDY ISN'T DISTURBED. THESE STORIES WERE ALL WRITTEN IN JEST.)

Contents

Introduction
1

Morning Rush
3

The Octopus Inspector
9

Psychic Fish
15

Opal and the Adult Babies
22

Apotemnophilia
31

Cannibal Requiem
37

Flags
43

Stiffy
54

An Exhumation of Eight Short Stories and Vignettes

INTRODUCTION

Let me start by saying thank you for taking some valuable time out of your day to spend perusing this book.

I deliberately decided to make them very short so that you could dip into it, choose a story to read, and then go about doing other things. I suspect that if you were to sit and read the entire book from cover to cover, you may be left with a sense of nausea or, worst-case scenario, fervent anger.

Actually, anger wouldn't be the worst-case scenario; indifference probably would be. I think

An Exhumation of Eight Short Stories and Vignettes

stories like the ones in this collection are written to stir some sort of emotion, regardless of the type.

So, I hope that if you do decide to read the entire book in one or two sittings, it makes you feel sick… or pisses you off to the point that you want to throw it across the room… or, better still, cast it into a raging holy fire whilst imploring benevolent spiritual forces to cleanse you from the words of a depraved, evil mind.

If you are of a similar disposition to myself, I hope you find the stories funny. I recall many moments during their composition when I was laughing out loud, in a room, alone.

I decided to form this collection as a challenge to myself. Creative writing is not as easy as some people think it is. I would urge anyone to give it a go though. Who knows what bizarre, horrifying, hilarious monsters lurk in the dark recesses of your own imagination? I, for sure, would be eager to meet them.

– Sean

An Exhumation of Eight Short Stories and Vignettes

MORNING RUSH

The Interviewee didn't realise there were still bits of subcutaneous fat from his husband's torso stuck between his teeth.

He had spent the majority of the morning grooming the dogs—a pair of French Bulldogs—named Pappy and Lazarus. The former had a tendency to be a little tearaway; Pappy would often have to be forcibly pinned down just to get a brush through her coat. Lazarus, like his namesake, would rise, albeit reluctantly, for food and walks; however, a congenital bladder problem would cause him to piss uncontrollably if made to stand still for any prolonged length of time.

Suffice to say, little morsels of yellow gristle remained stubbornly lodged between his molars, even though he brushed his teeth with the diligence and care of any ritual undertaken for the betterment of one's physical appearance and sense of self-confidence. Unfortunately, due to the time it took to get the dogs ready for the day, the Interviewee forgot to floss.

Waiting to be called into the office, the Interviewee's knee trembled. A lot of mental preparation had gone into these forthcoming moments: the assertive stride into the room, the correct amount of eye contact with the Interviewer from across the desk, and the firm-but-not-too-dominant handshake. Yet his knee continued to tremble, as if somewhere deep down in the cavernous dark, he had a feeling of diffidence about how this interview would go, and now that feeling stirred somewhere in that murky abyss, a dormant leviathan awoken from its slumber.

An anonymous voice clinically called out the Interviewee's name from the periphery, suddenly stopping the beast in its tracks. Without ruminating on how assertive his stride would appear to the squat, portly Interviewer who wore thick-lensed glasses—greatly enlarging his eyeballs so he looked like a balding tarsier—the

Interviewee found himself being drawn into the bright, artificial light, soon to be judged and, hopefully, welcomed into a corporate afterlife. At this moment, to be rejected and cast back to unemployment purgatory seemed a far worse fate. He sat down on a plain, unpadded chair, adjusting his posture slightly so his tense buttocks could find succour against the firmness of the base.

He had managed to pry loose a clump of fat with the tip of his tongue at some indiscernible moment between the waiting room and the office. He swallowed it, as the Interviewer sank into his chair opposite with the grace and poise of a dying game animal.

"And how did you find the journey in today?" the Interviewer asked with a feigned interest, apparent as the sweat stains on his white shirt which caught the Interviewee's eye.

The Interviewee pondered this question; not so much the question itself, but why people had an irritating tendency to begin a question with a conjunction. The quizzical look on the Interviewer's blanched face didn't register until an elongated strand of saliva broke from the corner of the Interviewee's mouth and landed onto his folded hands. He gazed up at the wall clock and realised that several minutes had passed since the Interviewer spoke.

"So, are you okay?" the Interviewer asked hesitantly. Conjunction yet again.

"Sorry. I don't quite know what happened…" the Interviewee replied, "…FUCK! SHIT! CUNT!"

"Pardon?" All the Interviewee could think of was how much of an efficient feigner the Interviewer appeared to him. He clearly did hear the barrage of curse words but, inexplicably, pretended not to.

"Sorry… I… err, um… I don't know why I… err… why I'm behaving like… like, this… really… I… err… am usually the epitome of… err… professional… professional-ism… professional-JISM!"

The hands of the wall clock were whirling fast now—a carousel of spokes chasing each other. Suddenly, it felt as if the temperature in the office had raised concomitant with the agitation beginning to cloak his vision like a warm blanket draped over his eyes.

"I suggest we terminate this interview. You clearly have no interest being here and, for reasons incomprehensible to me, are acting like a lunatic."

The Interviewer stood straight up from his chair and extended his fleshy hand forward.

Since the digits on the wall clock seemed to be slowly sliding down its face leaving trails of black ink, and the hands spinning incessantly, the Interviewee had no real awareness of how much time actually passed before he found himself in the empty office car park, blood that wasn't his spattered all over the front of his starched guayabera.

There were no shouts or screams emanating from the interior of the workplace, no security guards or police officers shouting forceful demands to *RAISE YOUR HANDS!* or *LIE FACE DOWN ON THE GROUND!* The Interviewee simply stood like a bloody life sculpture that had been placed impetuously in this empty space, in front of an automatic sliding door.

All he knew was that he would have chosen to wear a different style of shirt, and maybe a darker shade too, if he had sufficient time this morning to really consider his sartorial options.

Instead, his dogs needed to be groomed; the lifeless body of his husband cut up into pieces and eaten (he left the severed, chewy cock in the dogs' food bowls after splitting it along its length with a cheese knife so it could be evenly shared); and finally, there was a manic sprint to the bus stop in a meticulously polished pair of Loubs, just as he noticed the juddering carriage about to pull away from the kerb.

The Octopus Inspector

Madge didn't let the Inspector from the Environmental Health Agency into her house. Not because she was being obstinate but because she didn't have the strength or dexterity to climb over the mountain of debris that lay between her and the front door. She had been pinned to the stairs for five days now, under the weight of soiled adult nappies.

"Come through the fucking window, you idiot!" She tried to yell louder, but the sound that left her mouth was attenuated by the filthy mound pressed down on her chest.

"Mrs Oldham! Mrs Madge Oldham! PLEASE OPEN UP!" With his one good eye, the Inspector tried to peer through the small, coloured-glass panel near the top of the front door. It was impossible to see anything clearly due to all the years of dirt. "Please, Madge, OPEN THE DOOR!"

She squirmed, trying to pry her left arm free from under an old television set that had fallen at some point during the avalanche and landed onto her wrist. Being a frail, old lady, she heard the bones in her wrist crack before she felt the sudden whiplash of pain. As she moved, the roiling mass moved with her. She was disturbing the monster.

There was a continuous sound at the front door, and it aggravated her. The incessant tapping became a gradual pounding that reverberated through the mire, penetrating her bird-like skull. They were like hammer blows centring on a single point of her frontal lobe.

"Madge! Are you in there? I'm going to try the window! HOLD ON!"

If anyone happened to walk past her house at this moment, they would have seen a short, middle-aged man with gangly arms and a bulbous head clamber up a trellis, do a turn, a dive, then finally scale up a high barricade of plastic bottles filled with piss, just to get to a window that was slightly ajar. The octopus man did all this whilst clutching a clipboard.

Madge felt weak. She had eaten nothing for the last five days apart from a few smallish turds dislodged from the loosely wrapped nappies. They rolled across an undulating sea of crisp packets and ketchup sachets, stopping serendipitously a few millimetres from her head. By turning her head to the side and extending her tongue out as far as she could, she was able to manoeuvre the musky, dry clumps closer towards her mouth. She gulped them down like they were awful truffles.

"Hurry up and help me! I'm stuck!"

The Inspector had managed to open the window wide enough and scurry through into a room that *could* have been a bedroom. His eyes watered from the acrid stench of accumulated nastiness that began to waft out into the street.

The fumes and claustrophobia made him delirious. Trying to burrow through to reach the door was not easy, but to his surprise, his clipboard proved an adequate digging tool. He eventually grasped the doorknob with one hand, whilst steadied himself with his other. He pressed his hand down onto something moist and slippery. As he reflexively pulled his hand away, a peculiar membranous substance came away too, having stuck to his palm. He looked down and saw two glazed, gelatinous eyeballs protruding from a bloated, purply grey face staring back. The Inspector's revulsion and terror coalesced into a sudden gut punch that caused him to vomit over himself as he fled the room.

Fortunately, the landing was nowhere near as cluttered as the bedroom or the hallway where Madge was trapped in her excretal sarcophagus.

The Inspector stepped over vast mounds of rotten food encrusted into the frayed carpet. What appeared to be the glistening ribs and wet viscera of a putrefying pet—a cat or maybe a small dog—had become reanimated by a swirling cluster of maggots embedded in its chest cavity, spilling out, and blindly crawling onto and under the matted fur. It had become alive again. A ghastly, blotchy thing that seemed to move across the floor, towards the Inspector. He would have passed out right there if it wasn't for the ineffable stink that clawed at his nasal passages.

"MADGE! CAN YOU HEAR ME? ARE YOU OKAY?"

She looked towards the top of the stairs. The Inspector was in sight, soaked in golden puke and still holding his clipboard.

His good eye was directly on her. Madge twisted her neck to the oddest of angles and let out a sigh as she saw his malformed silhouette, upside down. The ceiling light had illuminated his enlarged head like a nimbus.

"MADGE!" The Inspector tripped over his own feet and tumbled down the stairs. He dropped to his knees and started scooping the assorted filth off Madge with his hands, then his clipboard, and finally, catapulted the television set almost across the entire length of the hallway and into the front door.

Madge gave a meek smile but enough to display her broken teeth, stained a brown hue from all the shit she had been eating.

"I'm so glad you're here. I thought I was going to die."

"It's all over now, Mrs Oldham. You're going to be fine."

"Thank God."

The Inspector emitted a sigh of his own. He wasn't sure whether he was going to tell his work colleagues the particulars of his afternoon visit.

"By the way…" Madge croaked listlessly, "…did you find my husband?"

An Exhumation of Eight Short Stories and Vignettes

P*SYCHIC FISH*

Tommy's Grandfather would do strange things with fish.

Their weekend escapades involved travelling to parts of the country in an ancient minivan, the backseats and floor space consumed by various apparatuses used—sometimes not used—for fishing. They would stop at lonely tea rooms on the way, make small talk with each other, as well as with the solitary characters they encountered who served them watery tea and desiccated biscuits.

When they arrived at wherever they were headed, Tommy and Grandfather would unload the minivan and proceed to stumble through bracken in early morning drizzle in order to reach a river, clumsily hauling with them an assemblage of rods and tackle boxes.

Grandfather would decide where they would settle for an entire day of fishing by unfolding his camping chair, gripping its arms and rigorously twisting, so that the chair's legs were wedged solidly into the ground. He performed this particular action *every* single time, as if he was asserting his claim over the land and adjacent waters through a demonstration of his physical strength.

Tommy didn't particularly enjoy these fishing trips with Grandfather. He only acquiesced because of Grandfather's tendency to supplicate him for company, which seemed rather pathetic and sad to Tommy. Grandfather was like an old, stray dog who was continually sniffing around his rubbish bins in the hope of finding some spoiled meat to alleviate an insatiable hunger.

Anyway, Tommy primarily indulged Grandfather because fishing gave them both plenty of time to do other things, whether that be sudokus, crosswords, or masturbating in the bushes. Sometimes, if they preferred, they would do nothing at all.

Grandfather would be the only one who caught fish on these trips. Tommy would gaze up from his phone and acknowledge the squirming object on the end of the hook, all wide-eyed and bewildered, with a nonchalant tip of his head.

Grandfather would manage to utter a breathy "Carp" or "Bream," due to his laryngectomy stoma being clogged up with yellowy mucus.

Tommy was admittedly fascinated by the deep well in Grandfather's throat, especially on the fishing trips where he got to see him perform a series of impromptu stunts such as lighting a cigarette; the filter held in position by constricting throat muscles.

Tommy's favourite act involved the fishing worms Grandfather preferred to use as bait instead of maggots. Tommy would be coaxed to choose a particularly long one and, at Grandfather's insistence, feed it carefully into the greasy chasm until it was most of the way in. Grandfather would then pinch his fingers and pull the entire worm back out of his throat hole whilst Tommy clapped and sang songs, the worm reminding him of the drawstring on his hoodie that he compulsively gnawed on and twisted around his index finger when he felt particularly anxious.

"Carp."

"That's great," Tommy replied. His apathy for Grandfather's catch made obvious for effect.

"This 'un's psychic." Grandfather managed to sputter the words out like a congested exhaust pipe.

"Huh?"

"Tells yer future, this 'un does."

Tommy was taken aback slightly by the fish Grandfather thrust in his face, speckles of river water landing on his cheeks. It still flapped from side to side, its mouth forming a Munchian scream.

"Okay, will you stop shoving it in my face please?"

"It's talkin' to yer, Tommy." It appeared as if Grandfather didn't hear—or was ignoring—Tommy's request.

Grandfather had his hand cupped under the fish's head and was squeezing its slippery jowls, manipulating the shape of its mouth whilst it continued to gasp futilely for air.

"Tom-meee. Tom-meee." Grandfather's raspy tone and twitching lips made him appear an unconvincing ventriloquist. Tommy pretended to laugh half-heartedly, a slight attempt to humour Grandfather so he could quickly get back to the porn on his phone.

"Tom-meee. Tom-mee. Lisss-unnnn. Dayn-jurrr."

Tommy couldn't rouse any enthusiasm within himself for this particular performance he'd not seen before. It seemed childish. He would rather see Grandfather do his smoking stunt again or extract a pulpy worm—currently coiled up in a Tupperware container—from that enthralling, little puncture in his gullet.

"Vuhhhh lyyyyyy-tt-zuh. Vuhhhh lyyyyy-tt-zuh. Tom-meee."

"Okay, you can quit pretending you caught a talking fish now."

Grandfather's eyes had rolled back in his head whilst his hand continually fondled the fish, which had finally stopped gasping.

"Hey! You hear what I said?" Tommy clutched Grandfather's arm and gave him a gentle shake.

"Huh?" Grandfather's pupils returned back to their correct position, like the spinning reels of a slot machine. He looked down at the prone fish in his possession for a moment, then chucked it into an open cooler.

Neither spoke for the rest of the day. No more fish were caught. Tommy's phone battery died. As the last vestige of the day's light disappeared, they retraced their steps through the bracken and finally arrived at the spot where the minivan was parked. Still without saying a word, they hauled their fishing gear into the interior of the vehicle and got into their respective seats. Grandfather turned the ignition, reviving the minivan back to life. Tommy was the first to break the silence: "Stick to pulling worms out the hole in your throat, okay?"

A heavy downpour had begun by the time they reached the first semblance of civilisation again. Tommy was in a half-sleep, his head colliding against the glass of the side window every time Grandfather forgot to avoid driving too fast over the many potholes in the road.

Grandfather strained to look through the veil of rainwater that defied the windscreen wipers' feeble attempt to bat it away. He could just about make out two undefined, blurry specks of light that seemed to be quickly increasing in size. Grandfather was scratching at his irritated throat;

the clogged stoma was causing his mouth to make the same gasping motion as the dead fish—recumbent in a weather-beaten cooler—had been making earlier.

Tommy's eyes fluttered open at the moment when he heard two discordant sounds permeate the enclosure around him: a frenzied beeping of a car horn and a familiar raspy pronouncement of "Vuhhhh lyyyyyy-tt-zuh…" emanating from either a cooler or Grandfather. He wasn't certain which, as the impact violently wrenched him back into a dark space.

OPAL AND THE ADULT BABIES

Opal tried not to wince as she suckled Rodger, a forty-five-year-old civil servant, who was already ten minutes over his allotted time. As he lay curled up into her, bald head rested in the crook of her numb arm, he made sounds reminiscent of a nuzzling piglet rather than the two-year-old he pretended to be during his lunch breaks twice a week.

She always tried to do right by her regular clients, and Rodger was one of her favourites, in that he always paid with new twenty pound banknotes and let her have some creative control over their scenarios. He made her laugh with his self-deprecating humour. He also had the bluest eyes, which were presently hidden from view by her large breast.

"Time's up, luv."

Rodger mumbled something, teeth still clenched onto Opal's dark, tender nipple.

"What did you say, luv?" More muffled sounds reverberated against her delicate skin. "I didn't hear what you said," Opal proclaimed.

Rodger reluctantly released his grip and looked up at Opal, beads of sweat trickling down his forehead and protuberant brow.

"I said five more minutes. You've got a good flow."

"Sorry, can't do, luv. You've already gone into overtime, I got two more clients this afternoon, and I'm dying for my lunch." She tenderly wiped his clammy head with the back of her smooth hand. Rodger's bottom lip began to tremble. Opal knew what was coming next—this was how he always forced himself to cry. "Come back tomorrow, and we can carry on where we left off. Don't you need to get back to work? Everyone will be wondering where you disappeared off to." She playfully pinched his lip, stopped it from quivering. Rodger let out a long sigh and then nodded reluctantly.

"Okay, Opal. Will you do one last thing before I go?"

"What, luv?"

"Change my nappy…" Rodger's voice suddenly transitioned into something resembling a confused fusion of baby gibberish and speech impediment, "…Eye diddy poopy poo. Eye got a durrty bum-bum."

She did this one last thing for Rodger so he could go back to the office reinvigorated and get through the next few hours without having to awkwardly change his own grubby nappy whilst standing up in one of the gents' stalls, and she could finally eat her cheese and pickle sandwiches, currently sat unclaimed at the back of the empty, communal fridge.

***

An hour or so later, Tony made his arrival known by pressing his finger down and holding it on the front entrance buzzer for an inordinately long time, even after the receptionist, Kara, had released the locking mechanism from where she sat at her desk.

Opal was getting herself refreshed in the bathroom, trying to wrest an ort of pickle from her front teeth with a toothpick when she heard a rap at her door. She discarded the toothpick and left the pickle where it was, as she went over to let Tony in.

She opened the door, which was painted a bright shade of pink, and greeted her client with a closed-mouth smile.

"Hello, Opal. How you been?" Tony's gruff baritone was chipped and flaky as the paint on the door panels. Before Opal could muster a terse response to his enquiry, he said: "Only fifteen minutes today. Got the kids in the car."

For the next quarter of an hour, Tony liked to imagine himself as a six-month-old baby. He had been coming to see Opal sporadically over the last few years—more so now but for shorter amounts of time—since his marriage was disintegrating and the kids were getting older and needed their dad to chauffer them places. This gave him a regular opportunity to stop by and see Opal for some much-needed *mummy and baby* time. He said to the kids, "No need to come in too. Just checkin' on my mate who's feeling a bit down in the dumps." He also claimed his mate needed to "borrow some dosh... he's broke," thus providing himself with an adequate alibi as to why there were *always* trips to the petrol station cashpoint on the way.

Opal didn't mind the fleeting incalls with Tony. He didn't require much encouragement to *get him off and out* again. He'd always undress from the waist down, revealing his cloth nappy held secure by an oversized safety pin and then lie down on the bed. He'd sink into the mattress due to his heavyset frame and start squirming on top of the beach towel that had been laid down over the satin duvet cover to collect any spillages.

After a few deep exhalations, Tony, the adult, would disappear, replaced by a babbling infant. He raised his arms and legs towards the ceiling, then waved and kicked uncoordinatedly about. This was Opal's cue to saunter over to the bed, uttering: "Hush, hush, little Tony, Mummy's here," retrieve the pacifier from her dressing gown pocket and tease it against his lips until he took hold of it.

Opal would then perch herself on the edge of the bed and rub and tickle his hairy gut, watching his flab and love handles jiggle, as she *cooed* and *aahed*. Tony would then suddenly sit up and insist they play *peek-a-boo* whilst he slipped his hand down into his nappy and masturbated, his face scrunched up and gurning, like he had a voice whispering into his ear, telling him how reprehensible this would all seem to his children, who were sat waiting impatiently in the back of his car.

After he was finished—and helped himself to an abundance of Opal's baby wipes for his hands—he would make a hurried beeline for the exit, saying no more than "bye" and almost stumbling down the steep, creaky staircase. Kara would watch him flee, not even checking that the front door had shut and locked properly on his way out.

**

Opal was glad Tony didn't stay long today. She was expecting a new client, and this was to be their inaugural session. She straightened the bed covers, lit a couple of scented candles to alleviate any lingering muskiness, and bent down to pick up the pacifier that had popped out of Tony's mouth mid-stroke like a bung that eventually succumbed to the increasing pressure that it was attempting to withstand.

Jimmy and Opal had been corresponding over the course of that same morning via text. His messages were pleasant-sounding enough. She even managed to chuckle to herself when his final sent text to her simply stated:

"I will bring lube. Lol. XXX"

She instantly replied:

"Haha. C u soon. X"

***

It was dark outside by the time there came a knock at the door. Opal had been sat cross-legged on the floor, her back against the bed, texting her daughter. Opal wanted to know if she was being good for Gemma, the babysitter; how her day at school had been; what she had for lunch; and whether Gemma had heated up the spaghetti that Opal had prepared the night before and left, wrapped in cling film, for her dinner.

Jimmy greeted Opal by tipping his burgundy fedora. In that briefest of moments, she absorbed all his outward affectations, as he brushed past her and appeared to glide into the room.

"Was it an hour you wanted, luv?"

He turned and said: "Indeed I do. I've got more money on me so I might choose to stay longer… but that depends on how things go."

Opal didn't feel particularly impressed or repelled by Jimmy. She had entertained clients before who possessed a similar suaveness and arrogance. Opal always found it amusing that despite all the bravado, underneath, they were all wearing adult-sized nappies—some even needed to have their bottoms wiped during their time together. Opal had worked in healthcare before; it wasn't a big deal. And the pay now was invariably better.

***

Opal watched the flames on the scented candles dance, casting ephemeral shadows against the wall. She could hear Jimmy whistling from behind the closed door of the en suite. He'd been in there a while, but that was fine; the meter was running, and she was being paid to wait.

The flames were hypnotic. Opal couldn't think of anything more elegant than their fluidity. They reminded her of her daughter practising for a dance recital in front of a mirror whilst Opal watched surreptitiously from the doorway.

Suddenly, a squeaky warble sounded from the threshold of the bathroom: a jarring shrill that clashed against the low murmur of traffic outside the window. It snapped Opal instantly out of her trance. It was Jimmy, putting on a voice that was not child-like or babyish. It didn't even sound human.

"I WANT TO BE A FOETUS!"

Opal couldn't quite process what he was saying.

"I WANT TO BE A FOETUS!"

Jimmy was standing against the backdrop of bathroom light, completely naked. Opal could see that there was a distinctive sheen covering his body from head to toe. His hair had been slicked back and was gleaming—globules of lubricant dripping from his limbs onto the carpet.

Opal's jaw slackened, and her eyes widened when they became transfixed onto the object that Jimmy was holding in his left hand. His grip on it was so tight that the serrated blade appeared to tremble, the candle flames casting glints of light onto the intimidating steel. Jimmy's breathing got heavier.

"I AM GOING TO BE A FOETUS!" he screeched at a terrified Opal, who was clutching the satin bed cover. His voice transitioned again so that every word of the next question felt like a tense stroke from the knife against her frozen skin: "Do you want me to try going in head first?"

APOTEMNOPHILIA

One of Sid's earliest childhood recollections was of masturbating to an amputee.

He had ripped a page out of one of his dad's dirty magazines stashed under the bed. He tried to remove the page so that it would have appeared—unless under careful scrutiny—that the magazine hadn't been tampered with. Unfortunately, the paper split right through the middle, crudely severing the woman's arm at the shoulder.

Sid was surprised by how aroused he suddenly felt staring at this modified image: the two pieces of paper positioned side-by-side, a slight gap between them, emphasising the detached sections of the woman's body.

***

He was sat slumped in the bath; the water lined up to his nose. His wrist still throbbed despite it having been several days. The doctor did mention the possibility of experiencing *phantom limb*, but this was more like pins and needles forming at the end of his forearm—now a stump, where his hand had been attached and was now just a memory.

Sid had not decided what body part to remove next; maybe one of his feet, *heck*, he might just take off the forearm that now didn't serve much purpose anyway. Either way, his decision would be the result of first figuring out the logistics of which piece of himself could be deemed expendable, without it causing him too much of a handicap. He was currently missing: an ear, the little finger of his left hand, and a quarter of his tongue, and he had pulled out most of his teeth.

He deliberated for a while longer whilst the bathwater gradually turned cold. He finally decided to remove the forearm. His feet were quite useful for getting in and out of the bathtub.

An Exhumation of Eight Short Stories and Vignettes

***

Sid ensured that the fridge freezer was full of ice packs and that there were plenty of clean towels on standby prior to any amputation. Cutting his hand off hadn't been too much of a problem—he had prepared by watching amateur videos of thieves being punished by *ISIS*.

Removing his arm at the elbow joint seemed a somewhat more intimidating challenge, due to the size of the radius and ulna in question. Detaching such a large section unnerved him more than usual. He had small hands, but his forearms were unnaturally long and thick. Kids used to call him *Popeye* at school.

He ultimately decided that he would apply a tourniquet using an old belt and then hack away at the joint with the sharpest chef's knife in the knife block. He would sterilise the blade as best as he could beforehand with boiled water. Sid was not too concerned. His phone would be next to him—fully charged—so that the emergency services could be contacted immediately after he ejaculated.

***

Sid emitted a tumultuous squeal through his clenched gums, a searing burst of pain resonating through his entire being. As soon as the knife pierced through soft tissue and struck bone, Sid knew immediately that he missed the spot he was aiming for. The point was lodged in the capitulum of his humerus, and Sid could not pull the blade back out however hard he tried.

A large pool of sticky crimson began to form and then ran down his quivering, useless forearm, onto the kitchen floor. His mouth let go of the worn leather belt, as he clasped onto the handle, twisting and pulling.

Soon an all-consuming layer of blackness descended over his vision like a hand portending a birthday surprise. The legs buckled from under him, and he collapsed and hit the ground hard before he even knew that he had fallen. His trousers and pants were already down around his ankles, for he liked to feel the warm, viscous semen shoot against his thighs. This time, however, it was only a warm feeling of piss.

***

Sid awoke, the knife still protruding from his arm. The pool of blood had become notably larger, deep red contrasting against pallid skin. Fortunately, the crude tourniquet had prevented him from completely bleeding out. He reached up to grab his phone from the countertop, still plugged in next to the laptop running continuous scenes of amputee porn. The four fingers of his only hand trembled as he dialled *999*.

***

He was sat slumped in the bath again. This time the water was shallow enough so he could toy with the coarse stitches embedded in his tender bicep. It felt nice. His mind was still consumed by fragmented images of flailing stumps, despite the dull ache that travelled from the bony end of his malformed appendage up to his clavicle.

He'd had accidents before—few as grievous as his most recent—Sid accepted that such things were bound to occasionally occur. In fact, the sense of danger titillated him as much as the act of amputation itself.

Thinking about it now, he could feel himself starting to get erect. Laying back and closing his eyes, he reached under the water to touch himself with his remaining hand whilst his other mangled limb rested on the edge of the bath like a bruised, eyeless seal basking on an acrylic rock.

For several minutes he struggled to achieve a climax, even when the vigorous thrusts caused water to splash repeatedly onto his face. Sid realised that he needed a more acute stimulus than just the internal slideshow of partial, anonymous bodies squirming about in his imagination. He released his grip and opened his eyes.

Sid looked intently at his toes which protruded out of the water, five little pink soldiers standing to attention.

Of course, removing a foot would be foolish. Especially, so soon after his mishap. The arm incident had shaken him more than slightly—he was prepared to admit that to himself. It was prudent, he decided, to save the bigger parts of his anatomy for when choice cuts began to dwindle. But surely, he could part with a few of the digits that he started to playfully wiggle about, causing small ripples to move across the surface of the water.

An Exhumation of Eight Short Stories and Vignettes

CANNIBAL REQUIEM

The Husband and the Wife sit opposite each other at a long, oak dining table. The centrepiece consists of a large, ornate silver platter; on display is a mixed selection of lightly grilled entrails whilst the upper section of an eviscerated cadaver—a naked man barely looking like a man at all—is prostrate on a custom-made six-foot-long chopping block. His glassy eyes stare vacantly, and portions of his face are missing. The gleaming bone and teeth show through the crudely made openings—an abundance of garlic butter sauce covering his waxy skin.

There is a palpable tension between them, embodied in a silence occasionally interspersed by the scraping of cutlery against plates and the clinking of wine glasses against decanters.

The Husband cuts into a thick piece of thigh. As the steak knife sinks deep into it, pink liquid oozes out of the meat and onto the china plate. He chews on a mouthful of succulent flesh cooked to his liking, whilst announcing, "The Chef did an excellent job with the *long pig* this evening."

The Wife ignores him and continues to eat slowly and deliberately, eyes looking down at the pieces of the cooked man's liver on her plate.

"Best we've had in a while, wouldn't you agree?"

The Wife lifts her eyes to look across at the Husband and lets out an audible sigh as if to make it obvious to him that this movement causes her a significant amount of exertion, and for the effort she expends, he should be grateful.

"You know I dislike it immensely when you talk with your mouth full. I've told you often enough."

The Husband swallows the meat down quickly, feeling chastised and somewhat embarrassed.

"Sorry, my dear. I'm sure you have informed me of your detestation for such habits *many* times." His cheeks become slightly flushed, and he tries to soften the increasing tension with a diversionary question: "Where is the Chef?"

"I gave him the rest of the evening off... because we need to talk."

"We do?"

The Wife puts down her knife and fork and gives the Husband a look that is one of both incredulity and disdain.

"Yes. We do."

The Husband shifts uncomfortably in his chair. The Wife notices this action.

"Are we just going to ignore the fact that this cancer eating away at me has metastasised? That it is far more aggressive than we have deluded ourselves into believing for so long? Are YOU really going to pretend that this is NOT the reality of the situation NOW?"

The Husband takes another bite of the thigh. He chews but suddenly the taste and texture of the dead man's leg seem to change, becoming far more bitter and tougher to swallow. He spits it out into his napkin.

"Some cartilage that wasn't removed. The Chef knows to be more careful."

The Wife realises that the Husband is not going to address the incontrovertible source of tension permeating the dining room like toxic smog, let alone help dissipate it through talking any more than he has to.

"Maybe I will ask the Game Keeper tomorrow if he can set some traps around the grounds and snare us a peasant child. He tells me he's seen more than usual roaming around the Estate recently. That always seems to be the case when we hold back their rations. They get hungry and start taking risks… and I know how much you particularly enjoy their tender meat. I will ask the Chef to make a stew… now the weather is getting colder. It will do your immune system good."

The Wife gazes at the Husband wearily for a moment before suddenly bursting into a torrent of tears.

The Husband, flummoxed, tries not to acknowledge the sobs coming loudly from the other end of the long table. He touches his cheek with the back of his hand. He can feel himself becoming flushed again.

"Oh... err... my dear... do you want something else to eat perhaps? Maybe one of the Chef's specials from the platter?"

This question causes the Wife's sobs to amplify to a hysterical pitch, before a surge of fury cuts through her wailing long enough for her to scream at the Husband: "WHAT IS WRONG WITH YOU?! I'M DYING, AND ALL YOU CAN ASK ME IS IF I WANT MORE TO EAT! YOU ARE A FOOL! AN INCONSIDERATE FOOL!"

Dumbfounded, the Husband gets up from his chair and walks hesitantly towards the Wife, who now appears to him like a wounded animal who could very well pounce and sink her fangs into his throat. He puts a hand on her shoulder—an unease preventing him from doing anything other than pat her gently. He doesn't look at her but instead at the carcass smeared in a buttery sauce.

"I understand that YOU must be feeling somewhat perturbed by the news YOU received today... no use dwelling on such dismal reports though. Doesn't do the heart, or the digestion, much good. Anyway, I'm sure cures are always found for this sort of thing... for the affluent and those of good social standing anyway... Wine?"

Lachrymose, the Wife quietly utters without looking up, "Go back to your seat and sit down."

The Husband complies. He just wants to get through the rest of dinner without any more fuss if at all possible.

He picks up his cutlery and proceeds to carve up more meat when, without thinking, blurts out: "Even if the prospect of the Doctors finding a cure for YOUR illness is unlikely, YOU will eventually come to terms with that fact… being the reasonable woman that you are."

The Husband emits a buffoonish guffaw if only as a reflexive response to assuage a tense atmosphere that he finds most disagreeable at dinner time.

Silently, the Wife gets up from her chair and walks towards the Husband. She's petite and dainty but strides assertively and with a purpose. She appears in stark contrast to the masticating oaf who stops midway through eating a piece of a dead man impaled on the tines of his fork, whose eyes widen in complete surprise as she rams her steak knife deep into his chest.

An Exhumation of Eight Short Stories and Vignettes

FLAGS

Mr Kindsay was never keen on Christmas. As he grew older and became increasingly cantankerous, he disliked it even more. When the young family moved in opposite him a couple of years ago and immediately began engaging in extreme outdoor displays to arouse some festive cheer among the local residents of Cedarwood Way, he decided that Christmas was *just for cunts*.

Nigel, the patriarch, would spend most of the year planning the ostentatiously large dioramas and full-scale nativity scenes, engineering a light show that worked in synchronicity with Christmas holiday music. There would be an inflatable Santa

Claus propped up against the chimney, candy cane fences lining the driveway, and an invariable scattering of fake pine trees saturated in multicoloured baubles over the front lawn.

Mr Kindsay hated all of it. The thing he hated most was seeing all the other neighbours swooning around Nigel in the middle of the street, mouths agape as they stared in ridiculous wonderment at the elaborate exhibition. And Nigel would relish it. He would take a bow and bask in their adulation like he was the *King of Cedarwood Way*. Mr Kindsay would sneer at them all from behind his living room curtain whilst he muttered *what a sad bunch of mongoloid cunts* under his tobacco-infused breath.

***

Sometimes, when the weather was warmer, an ice-cream van would park up right outside Nigel's house. As it filled the air with a repetitive melody, alerting everybody in close proximity to its arrival, the family would rush out of their front door and gambol towards it—father, mother, a prepubescent boy and girl—squealing and hyper with delight.

Mr Kindsay, alarmed by the high-pitched racket, would jump out of his chair and quickstep over to the window to investigate the commotion. He was unsure of what he expected to see, but he hoped it would be a gory sight: Nigel's wife, Fiona, twisted and mangled under an axle. Maybe the two kids, crumpled and broken, their little bodies having experienced the bludgeoning impact of the ice-cream van, as it knocked them off their bikes. Most of all, he wanted to see Nigel on his knees, eyes tightly closed and mouth wide open, locked in a silent scream of uttermost anguish.

This fantasy would cause Mr Kindsay to chuckle to himself until he sputtered and coughed up a wad of thick, verdant-coloured phlegm into his hand.

***

As soon as the television adverts began to chime that *holidays are coming*, Mr Kindsay knew that Nigel would soon be out there on the lawn setting up his display. It would take most of a day to get everything prepared, and there it would remain for a full month, at least, drawing spectators from even a few of the other nearby streets.

Mr Kindsay thought that the garish display was a pathetic attempt to gain adoration and favour with the neighbours. He never wanted compliments. He never bothered anyone. Only exception was the old lady, Miss Mudge, who used to live next door. She would always take such a long time answering her door or walking to her front gate, despite the use of a walking aid. For some reason, he couldn't quite fathom, her glacial pace would bother him immensely. He would be smoking or pissing outside when he'd turn, and she would be there—moving along the row of rose bushes like a wrinkly, grey-haired snail—*tut-tutting* at him.

One night, under the camouflage of darkness, Mr Kindsay sneaked over to next door so he could peer through her window. Another night, he noticed she had fallen and lay prone on the kitchen linoleum floor. She was squirming and barely able to make a sound. A few nights later, he saw that she was still squirming. A few more nights passed, and he saw that she finally stopped.

***

Around noon, Mr Kindsay was leant up against the door frame of his front entrance, smoking. He was observing Nigel and a couple of his *dopey, mongo mates* on the roof. They were struggling to install a huge neon sign that said "JOY TO THE WORLD" onto the sloped surface. Even though the sign was cumbersome and heavy, the three friends were laughing uproariously, as if what they were attempting to do was suddenly the funniest thing in the world.

Their laughter bothered him. He felt that it was the laughter of imbeciles. He envisioned them for a moment as *pinheaded retards* rocking back and forth whilst a frumpy nurse in a starched white dress and cap fed them spoonfuls of jelly.

Fiona was looking up at them from below; her hand pressed against her mouth. She was trying desperately to stifle her own laughter. And the fact that she wasn't just letting her laughter out bothered him too.

Mr Kindsay felt his stomach churn at the sight of it all. He flicked his cigarette butt over into next door's garden—*Miss Mudge would be tut-tutting about that if she was still alive*—and trundled back into his house, slamming the door behind him.

***

By late afternoon, Nigel's Christmas display was near completion. The light show had yet to be switched on, but the rotund Santa Claus and all the rest of the inflatable decorations were in their allocated places. The nativity scene—consisting of a wooden stable, fibreglass animals, wise men, and enamoured parents looking down at a baby Jesus in a crib—took up most of the frontage. The entire spectacle was to be illuminated by strategically placed garden spotlights. Mr Kindsay hated that baby Jesus. He was repulsed by the abnormally large head, which made it look like *the daft fucker* had *water on the brain*.

***

Mr Kindsay was relieving himself in the bushes when he noticed Nigel's two children walking down Cedarwood Way. They were on his side of the street, making their way towards his house. Typically, he would scurry back inside before they came too near—he couldn't stand being around children for *any* length of time. This time, however, something compelled him to stay where he was.

He hastily zipped up the fly of his trousers, disregarding the wet patch on his crotch which would usually have aroused him to anger. As soon as the children, in their school uniforms, were a slight distance away from him and about to cross over to the other side of the street, he found himself calling out, "Hey, kids! Did you 'ave a good day at school?"

The children looked curiously at Mr Kindsay. They weren't frightened of him. In fact, they had never even seen him before now. Nigel and Fiona had never mentioned him. They had never even thought about him for more than a few fleeting moments. Usually, when they did, it was around this time of year when the residents of Cedarwood Way stepped out of their houses to admire the Christmas display. Most of the neighbours would tell Nigel how much they admired his enthusiasm for the holiday and for bringing some fun to the, otherwise quiet, street. It was only the old man who lived across from them that never did.

They thought he was a bit eccentric and reclusive, but that wasn't necessarily a bad thing. Some old people just had their *funny ways*. All Nigel and Fiona knew of him was that his name was "Kindsay" and that he had been a sailor... or in the Navy... *something to do with boats or ships*. Mr Bullard, a retired accountant who lived with his wife adjacent to Nigel and was himself recently deceased, only mentioned all of this once in passing.

The boy eventually spoke, whilst his sister looked away shyly.

"Yes, thank you."

"I've seen you two before. You live across the street from me. I saw your daddy and his friends putting up the Christmas decorations. They look... lovely."

The boy plucked up the courage to confidently proclaim, "We have the best-decorated house in the entire street!" The girl giggled.

"And Dad says, he's going to make it even bigger and better every year!"

Mr Kindsay swallowed some bitter sick that had arisen in the back of his throat.

"Sounds... great." He wasn't sure if that sounded the least bit genuine.

"Dad says, you were a sailor?"

It was Mr Kindsay's turn to look at his interlocutor with curiosity. Only his look was tinged with a slight air of annoyance.

"He did, did he? Well, that's true. I used to be a signaller during my days at sea. Waving flags to communicate with other ships, that sort of thing. Semaphore. That's what it's called." He noticed that he had both their attentions now. "Flags are a great way of getting your message across without actually having to speak."

Whilst the boy imagined naval battles and cannons blasting, Mr Kindsay became aware that the girl was playfully hopping from one foot to the other.

"I got my old handheld flags inside. Got a whole collection I 'ave. Want to see them? Then you can tell your parents all about Mr Kindsay's flags. I could even teach you both how to spell your names just by waving flags about. I reckon your daddy would love that."

***

By late evening, Mr Kindsay heard Nigel and Fiona standing outside in the street. Their distressed voices merged with a chorus of others. He assumed they belonged to residents who had now stepped out of their houses not to praise Nigel but to console him and tell him and his wife that they should *try not to worry too much about those little lost ducklings.*

As evening turned to night, the blue flashing lights of a police car bounced off Mr Kindsay's bedroom wall. He lay in bed, arms behind his head, grinning into the darkness.

***

As morning arrived, Nigel and Fiona were sat embracing each other in their living room, both bleary-eyed from lack of sleep. Empty cardboard boxes lay scattered about, the words written upon them in Sharpie, such as DECORATIONS / TINSEL / FAIRY LIGHTS, now devoid of all meaning.

The sound of the doorbell suddenly resonated through the whole house. Nigel got up to answer it. It was Mrs Bullard from next door, ashen-faced, and barely able to speak. Nigel could hear the murmuring of other people at a short distance behind her. Some appeared to be crying.

Fiona could hear it too. She came to the door, and Mrs Bullard turned from Nigel to her—a look of despair in her eyes, as achingly real as their missing children. Mrs Bullard looked like she had seen a horror that there were simply no words for. She moved aside.

Nigel and Fiona immediately noticed a crowd standing outside Mr Kindsay's house. There were two, long wooden flagpoles rooted into the soil of his front garden. They tracked the length of the poles until they reached the top, at which point both Nigel and Fiona released a resounding scream in unison.

Nigel fell to his knees, pulling Fiona down on top of him. Hanging to the flagpoles were two body-length pieces of peeled skin—the size of a boy and a girl. What were once arms and legs flapped about in the early morning breeze, and the faces now contained holes instead of eyes.

STIFFY

"YOU CAN'T GET FUCKING HARD! WHAT'S WRONG WITH YOU?!"

Ron was in the bathroom, scolding himself in front of the mirror above the sink. He was getting so irate; he started hitting himself in the penis. Doreen was listening to him from the bedroom. She was sprawled out on the bed, staring up at the ceiling and thinking to herself: *Great, here he goes again...*

***

For the last several months, it had been one failed attempt after another. They had tried so many things that it was *now all just a blur*. There were pills bought off the internet, ancient herbal remedies, and advice from doctors, friends, and therapists. There were new-age medicine and old wives' tales. The blue pills prescribed by his long-suffering doctor did as much use as travel mints. When they increased the dosage, Ron once passed out as soon as he strode into the bedroom, naked except for some black, cowhide riding chaps.

Doreen tried her best. Sometimes, she would try on an assortment of lingerie; other times, she would wear nothing at all. She play-acted being coy with Ron and, then when that failed, played demanding. She bought a panoply of sex toys: dildos, anal plugs, ball gags, leather whips— an esoteric mixture of contraptions and devices that would have been familiar to the likes of *Heinrich Kramer*. None of it did much good. Ron would just end up lying on top of her, squirming like a caught fish and cursing himself for having a *dead cock.*

***

Several hours into their latest evening whilst the kids were away for the night with friends, Doreen found herself scouring the web for potential ideas. She stumbled upon a website describing the efficacy of role play and fantasy re-enactment, in revitalising the sex lives of couples that had gone tepid. Her lower region felt sore and hot; Ron had ended up rubbing her raw, so she kept crossing and uncrossing her legs, unable to find a comfortable position, as she sat on Ron's office chair.

She considered this another avenue to try the next time they mutually felt up to the challenge. It couldn't hurt to give role play a go. Various possible scenarios began to race through Doreen's mind the more she warmed to the idea and even got a little bit excited too. Maybe Ron's fantasy would be of Doreen as a seductive boss who demanded that he helped alleviate her stress over a looming project deadline. Or maybe he would want her to be a naughty schoolgirl, sent to the headteacher for some much-deserved corporal punishment. *Yes*, she decided, *role play was definitely worth a try.*

***

After having explained to Ron the details of her venture into investigative research, she found that he was surprisingly pliable to a brainstorming session, in which they conjured up some scenarios that they could try out together. He had pummelled his private parts and his self-confidence aplenty, so he was willing to accept any and all suggestions, however weird or unconventional they might be.

To be fair, Ron hadn't been forthcoming with many ideas. He just wasn't the creative type. However, Doreen could sense that he was ruminating about something.

"What is it, hun?"

Ron took a deep intake of breath, then opened his mouth to speak.

"I have a scenario in mind, but I'm not sure if you're going to like it. I think it could work, or at least, be something worth trying."

"Tell me then."

"You could... erm..." Ron scratched his fuzzy, greyish beard, "...pretend to be dead."

"What do you mean? Like a zombie? That's hilarious."

"No. I mean, *play dead*. You know, lie there, like a dead body."

"I'm not sure I understand," Doreen replied. It was all she could say to prevent herself from being speechless at her husband's suggestion.

Ron began to get more animated with every new detail of his idea, which seemed to roll off his tongue and collide into Doreen, making her increasingly uncomfortable.

"We could do you up in white make-up, you know, *corpse paint*. Make it look like all the colour has been drained from you. Or green make-up. Make it look like the rot has started to set in."

Doreen thought Ron had to be joking. There were suggestions in the past that he wasn't particularly in favour of—the one where Doreen suggested he be cuckolded by the bullish Nigerian who ran the newsagents being a particularly notable one.

"Okay, haha. It was just a suggestion. If you don't think it's a good idea, just say. You don't have to poke fun."

"This IS my suggestion. I really, REALLY think we should give it a go."

"Hun, that sounds… warped."

"I know, it's absolutely mad, but we've tried damn near everything else. Let's just do this and see. Please. I'm desperate."

***

They managed to alter Doreen's appearance rather convincingly. Together they had gone to a party shop and bought a vast array of make-up kits, finally settling on her looking like a *mouldering corpse that had been found in a river*. Ron had spent the early part of their evening looking up photographs of drowning victims on his phone. Doreen couldn't stomach that sort of thing so she resorted to having a long soak in the bath before the make-up was to be applied.

Now with the transformation complete, she looked more appropriate for Halloween than an evening of intimate relations with her husband.

Doreen insisted that she wear her new silk negligee, rather than the assortment of tattered, moth-eaten clothes Ron had picked up outside a charity shop on their way home. Despite his incessant pleading, that was one thing she would not agree to. He eventually did yield, after some remonstration like a sulky teenager.

***

She was waiting on top of the bed covers, when Ron came in from the bathroom wrapped in a beige towel. He preferred to keep his vest on, since he was self-conscious about his sagging gut and soft pecks—drooping down on his chest like the sorrowful eyes of a bloodhound.

Doreen saw her husband in a different light during moments like this. He seemed vulnerable and scared. If this evening wasn't supposed to be about one kind of physical affection, she would have happily embraced him and let him blubber like a small child in her *decay-coloured* arms.

***

A few minutes later, Ron was on top of Doreen, inadvertently breathing and wheezing in her face, thrusting blindly at her crotch. The *blacks and greens* were already beginning to smear, staining the pillowcases, her negligee, and Ron's white vest. He was doing his best to clear his mind of all distractions and focus on only *wetness…* and *pink, moist, fleshy* things… *tight apertures* closing around his… *dead cock.*

Ron stopped his futile attempt. No movement from below.

"It's no good. Nothing's working."

Doreen's Halloween make-up made her look less like a cadaver now, and more like a woman who sported a smudged, full body and face tattoo created with prison ink.

"Give it a bit longer, hun. There's no rush."

"It's no use. I'm…" Doreen put her finger to Ron's lips.

"...Give it a bit longer, hun. Now... fuck me," she interjected seductively.

Ron, ambivalent about this continued pretence, obliged. He returned to thrusting but now only half-heartedly. Doreen, always the devoted wife, pretended that it felt like something other than bone hitting against bone. She moaned: "That's it, Ron! That's it! Give it to me! Harder!"

He knew that she was doing all this for him, but he couldn't help feeling as if her carnal affectations were, in an obtuse way, somewhat belittling.

"That's it! Fuck me, Ron!"

He began to plunge harder and more forcefully at Doreen, as her moans of pleasure became siren calls, and their bodies became blunt instruments of ineffectuality.

"Fuck me, Ron! Fuck me! C'mon, Ron, fuck me!"

Ron's eyes were shut tight. He was still trying to picture something, *anything*, that stirred his loins. As he did so, he suddenly realised Doreen's hands were scratching at his face.

He was smothering her with a pillow—her exhortations muted by his bodyweight pressed down on her head. Wailing arms reached about, only managing to clutch at the air. Ron wasn't thrusting anymore. Even when he opened his eyes and realised what was happening, he continued to hold down the pillow with even more resoluteness than before.

Doreen's arms eventually went limp and dropped to the mattress. All became quiet and still. Ron kept the pillow firmly over his wife's face.

As the seconds turned into minutes, Ron began to sense something rousing below the covers. With his free hand, he explored in the darkness. Doreen was still hot, and he was getting... *hard*. Ron could also feel his heart thumping from under his vest.

Finally, he moved the pillow aside, to see Doreen's painted face—her eyes closed, her jaw slack. Ron kissed her tenderly on the lips. He was *stiff* now, more rigid than he could *ever* recall being. With a slight flex of his hip, Ron was now inside his wife. It felt safe and secure in this place. He wanted to remain there forever.

ABOUT THE AUTHOR

Sean has an appreciation for both extreme horror movies and literature. He lives in the South West of England with his girlfriend, their daughter, two cats, and a tortoise. This is his first collection of stories.

Made in United States
Troutdale, OR
11/17/2023

14675835R00043